DATE DUE

OCT 13 '80	102	APR 05 1982
MAR 2 9 1982	102	
FEB 2 2 1983	201	
OCT 2 4 1984	201	
OC 02 '85	201	
OC 16 '85	301	
OC 23 '85	301	
OC 29 '85	301	
AP 09 '87	201	
AP 23 '87	201	
AP 30 '87	201	
MY 07 '87	201	
MY 1 4 '87	201	
MY 28 '87	201	
JE 04 '87	201	
AP 27 '99	183	
JA 18 '00	483	
AP 27 '0		
GAYLORD		PRINTED IN U.S.A.

CHAMELEON WAS A SPY

Story and Pictures by Diane Redfield Massie

Thomas Y. Crowell   New York

Library of Congress Cataloging in Publication Data

Massie, Diane Redfield. Chameleon was a spy.
SUMMARY: Chameleon becomes a spy in order to recover
the formula for the world's best pickles.
[1. Chameleons—Fiction. 2. Pickles—Fiction.
3. Spy stories] I. Title.
PZ7.M42385Ch 1979   [Fic]   78-19510
ISBN 0-690-03909-3   ISBN 0-690-03910-7 lib. bdg.

FIRST EDITION

For Shansi

Chameleon liked to change colors.
He could match the rug and the chair.

He could match the walls and the curtains.
"I can match anything," said Chameleon.
"You name it."

It was hard for his mother
to find him, even upside down
in the parlor. "CHAMELEON!"
she would call next to him.
"WHERE *ARE* YOU?"

Chameleon practiced every day, changing his colors from red to green, or from pink to purple and blue.
He could manage every color in the rainbow, adding dots and stripes and even zigzags when necessary.

"I shall be a spy when I grow up," said Chameleon.
"No one will ever catch me."

One day, as he was reading the papers, he noticed a small advertisement. "WANTED," it said, "RELIABLE PERSON FOR SUPER SECRET WORK. Apply at: 222 South Bean Street."

"How exciting!" said Chameleon, leaning against the refrigerator. He turned as snowy white as the door just for practice.

"Chameleon," said his mother. "Where *are* you?"

"I'm going to get a job," said Chameleon, becoming as yellow as the wall. "Wish me luck."

"Good luck," said his mother. "Is that you by the door?"

Chameleon waved good-bye and rushed outside.

He ran down the road to town, turning green and brown to match the countryside.

At last he came to town.
He went into the post office.
"Where is South Bean Street?"
he asked.

"Two streets over," said the postmaster.
"Who said that?"

Chameleon walked down South Bean Street. He stopped
before Number 222.
    THE PLEASANT PICKLE CO.
said a sign overhead.
    Chameleon knocked loudly.
The door opened.

"Who's there?" said a voice.

"It's Chameleon," said Chameleon, turning as brown as the door.

"Where?" asked the voice.
"I don't see anyone!"
A man with a bushy beard looked
out. He stared up and down
the street.

"I'm right here," said Chameleon,
waving his arms.

"GOOD HEAVENS!" said the man,
"A FROG!"

"I'm *not* a frog," said Chameleon. "I'm a chameleon."

"What do you want?" asked the man.

"A job," said Chameleon. "What's the super secret work?"

"I can't tell you," said the man. "Follow me."

Chameleon followed him down a long hall, which led to an office. They went inside.

"Gentlemen," said the man, bowing. (Nine men and a potted plant sat around a long table.) "May I present Mr. Chameleon."

"Where *is* he?" asked the Chairman of the Board.

"He's right here, somewhere," said the man with the bushy beard, looking about.

"Here I am," said Chameleon. He leaped onto the table.

"A FROG?" said everyone.

"I am a chameleon!" said Chameleon loudly. "And I am here to apply for the super secret job."

The Board Chairman cleared
his throat. "Aaaheeemmmmmmmmm."
Everyone stared at Chameleon.

"This is highly irregular," said the Chairman.
"We did not expect *chameleons* to apply for this highly
secret work."

"What kind of work *is* it?" asked Chameleon.

The board members looked at each other.

"Spying," said the Chairman.

"WOW!" said Chameleon.

"Pleasant Pickles have always been the best!"
announced the Chairman, pounding his fist on the table.
The coffeepot rattled and the rubber plant shook.
"But *now*..." He blew his nose on his handkerchief
and dried his eyes on his sleeve.

"The Perfect Pickle Company will make *better* pickles than
we do," whispered the man with the bushy beard.
"Really?" said Chameleon.
"THEY HAVE *OUR* SECRET FORMULA!" shouted the Chairman.
"THEY'VE STOLEN IT!"

"How?" asked Chameleon.

"A pickle scientist took it," said the man with the bushy beard. "He works for the Perfect Pickle Company."

"WE MUST NOT BE SECOND BEST!" cried the Chairman. "WE MUST GET OUR FORMULA BACK!"

"I'll get it," said Chameleon.

"You?" said the Chairman. "I don't mean to be rude, but how could a puny little Chameleon get back our precious pickle formula? HA! HA! HA!"

Everyone laughed.

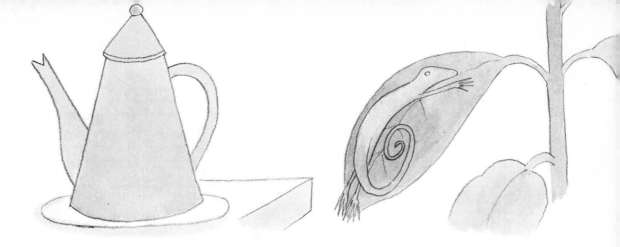

Chameleon leaped to the rubber plant.
He turned as green as a leaf.

"Where is he?" asked the board members.

"Here I am," said Chameleon. He jumped
off onto the coffeepot. His skin was a coppery
orange. "Guess where I am *now*," he said.

The board members hunted about the room,
looking under their chairs.

"Where is he? I don't see him. Can you
find him? I can't," they said.

"Well," said Chameleon. He leaped back to the table again. "What do you say?"

"INCREDIBLE!" cried the Chairman. "YOU'RE HIRED!"

"A perfect spy," said the others. "Chameleon will get that formula!"

The next day, Chameleon rode in a taxi to the Perfect Pickle Company factory. His driver let him out.

"Wait here," said Chameleon. He went inside, sliding along the pale tan walls, matching them perfectly.

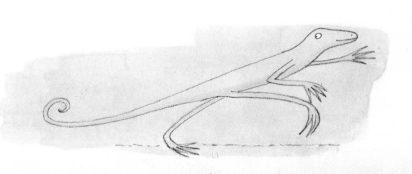

LABORATORIES said a sign on a door.
Chameleon opened it. He saw tables and
bottles and jars. There were tubs
of pickles sitting everywhere.
"This must be where they make
the formula," he said.
He waited next to a tub.

Soon a scientist in a long white coat came in.
His beard was pale orange. It hung down to his buttons.
"Now that *I* have the Pleasant Pickle formula," he wheezed,
"Pleasant Pickles will soon
go out of business!
Hee, hee, hee!"
He sprinkled a bit of salt
in the pickle tub next
to Chameleon.

"THE PERFECT PICKLE COMPANY WILL MAKE
MILLIONS!" he shouted, "MILLIONS!"

"Good heavens!" said his assistant,
coming in the door. "Is anything wrong?"

"WRONG?" roared the scientist.
"HOW CAN ANYTHING BE WRONG, YOU BOTTLE-BRAIN!
WE HAVE THE FORMULA!"

"Where is it?" asked his assistant.

"Here!" said the scientist, flinging it down
on the table. "No one else shall ever see it!"

S E C R E T

1 bushel cucumbers
(soaked in salty brine)

1 large horseradish
2 gallons vinegar
8 celery seeds
4 dill blossoms
AND 1 cup mustard,
made with
crinkleroot juice

S E C R E T

Chameleon slid around the pickle tub.
He could see the formula. It was next to
the scientist's hand. He turned his skin
white as the table, and crept slowly out.

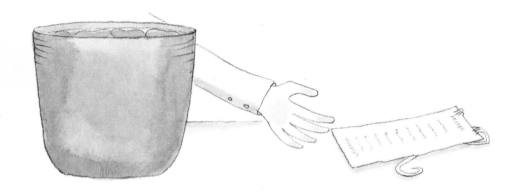

The scientist reached for the formula.
Chameleon slipped underneath and clung
to the top.
"What's this?" said the scientist,
turning the paper over.
Chameleon flipped over to the front side,
and the formula fell to the table, CLUNK!

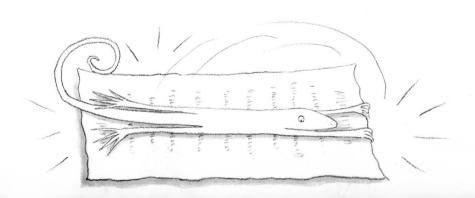

Chameleon slid to the bottom and lay still. His skin matched the words underneath him perfectly.

"Crinkleroot juice," they said.

AND 1 cup mustard,

made with

crinkleroot juice

SECRET

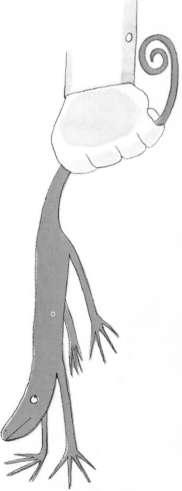

"WAIT!" snapped the scientist, staring at the page. "Eyes are looking out of the formula!"

"Eyes?" said his assistant.

"Quiet, lettuce-head! I must get to the bottom of this!" His hand closed over Chameleon.

Chameleon turned green as a pickle.

"AHA!" cried the scientist, holding Chameleon by the tail. "What have we *here*?"

"It's a pickle," said the assistant.

"It's a frog," said the scientist.

"I'm a chameleon," said Chameleon.

"WHAT," roared the scientist, "are you doing here?"

"Just looking around," said Chameleon. He stared at the formula beneath him as he swung back and forth.

"You were reading the secret formula!" said the scientist. "YOU ARE A SPY!"

Chameleon twisted loose and leaped to
the table. He snatched the secret formula
up, and jumped down to the floor.

"WHERE IS HE?" shouted the scientist.
"He's crawling out the door," said
the assistant.
"AFTER HIM!" cried the scientist.
"HE MUST NOT ESCAPE!"

Chameleon ran down the hall. The door at the end said
PICKLING PLANT. He hurried inside.

There were tubs of pickles everywhere, pickles steaming
in brine. Chameleon ran up a ramp. He could see
the conveyer belts below with bottles riding along them.
The bottles were passing under a chute which filled them up
with pickles.

"STOP HIM!" shouted the scientist, rushing through
the door.

Chameleon leaped to the pickle
chute. But his foot slipped.
Down, down, down, he fell.
    PLUNK! into a bottle.
    Pickles poured down
from the pickle chute.
    "HELP!" yelled Chameleon.
    Pickles surrounded him,
and one lay on his head.
The formula sank to the bottom.
    "HELP! HELP!"

CLAMP! went the lid on the bottle.

SWUP! went the label in front.

"HELP! HELP!" yelled Chameleon inside the bottle.

But no one heard him.

Chameleon rode down the conveyer belt. He pushed up his lid just a crack.

"Number 936,073,492," said the checker at the end of the line.

Chameleon waved his arms. But his bottle moved into a box with eleven other bottles, all filled with pickles.

PERFECT PICKLE
COMPANY

The box lid came down, FLUMP!
It was very dark.
"I'm not a pickle," said Chameleon
to himself. "I'm a chameleon."
He settled himself on top of a pickle
and dozed in the darkness.

After a very long time, Chameleon
felt himself tipping back and forth.
The pickles bumped against him,
and the pickle juice sloshed against
his chin. "We're moving somewhere,"
he said.
THUMP!

Creeeeet, creeeet, pop! The box lid
came off, letting bright daylight in.
Chameleon covered his eyes. It was
much too bright to see.
Slosh! Slosh! went the pickle juice.
The pickles bumped his sides.
CLUNK! CLUNK! Then everything was still.

Chameleon uncovered his eyes. He saw rows and rows of cans and jars, sitting on long shelves. "Where am I?" he said.

An old man passed him, pushing a basket. He stopped in front of the pickles.

"I'm in a market!" cried Chameleon. He waved his arms and pounded on the glass.

But the old man didn't see or hear him. He pushed his basket slowly away.

Chameleon pushed hard on the lid above him, but he could not widen the crack. "This is terrible!" he said. "I could wait on this shelf for months before someone buys me!" He bit off a piece of pickle and chewed it slowly, thinking.

"I'll turn bright red," he said. "*Then* someone's sure to notice me." He turned his skin crimson and moved about, waving his arms and legs.

"Mommy," said a little girl. "Look at that funny pickle."

"What pickle?" said her mother, reading her market list. She picked up Chameleon's jar and dropped it into her basket.

"Thank heavens!" said Chameleon. "Saved at last!"

"Let me see the pickle," said the little girl.

"Don't bother me," said her mother, reading her list.

A large bag of noodles dropped into the basket.
It lay over Chameleon's jar.

"Pickles and noodles," said her mother. "Now we can go
to the checkout counter."

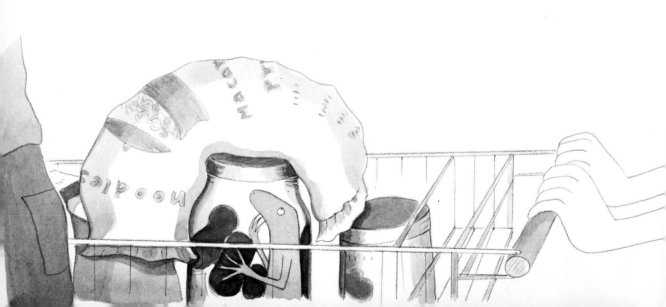

They moved quickly to the front of the store.
"Next," said the manager.

Chameleon's jar sat on the counter. The clerk
picked it up. Chameleon waved and smiled.

"Eeeeeeeeeeeeeeeekkk!" shrieked the little girl's
mother. "WHAT'S THAT?"

"GOOD HEAVENS!"
shouted the manager.
"I'LL CALL THE
FOOD INSPECTOR!"

The food inspector arrived in a rush.
"A CONTAMINATED BOTTLE OF PICKLES!" he announced.
"THIS BOTTLE IS NOT FIT FOR HUMAN CONSUMPTION!
IT SHALL BE CONDEMNED!"

"Let me out!"
shouted Chameleon.
    But no one heard him.

    The photographers came from
the paper. They photographed
Chameleon's jar.
    Someone put the jar in a bag and carried it
off to the police station.

"PERFECT PICKLE CO. CLOSED!" said the papers the next day.
"A CONTAMINATED JAR OF PICKLES IS FOUND ON A MARKET SHELF.
THE PUBLIC IS OUTRAGED."

"Good heavens!" said Chameleon's mother
when she saw the paper that morning.
She hurried down to town.
"LET MY SON OUT OF THAT JAR!"
she said.

The Police Chief pried off the lid.

"Thank you," said Chameleon,
dripping pickle juice over the desk.
He followed his mother out the door
and hurried home.

"Chameleon," said his mother at breakfast,
"how did you like your new job?"
"It was all right," said Chameleon,
"if you like being a pickle."

The telephone rang.
"Hello?" answered Chameleon.

"I've read the morning paper,"
said the Chairman of the Board.
"Good work!"

"Thank you," said Chameleon.

"Did you get the formula…?"

"Yes," said Chameleon.

"YAHOOOOOOOOOO!"
yelled the Chairman
into the receiver.

"I'll be right down," said Chameleon.

He hurried down to 222 South Bean Street.

A taxi drove past. "Hey," yelled the driver,
"you never came out of that place! Where were you
anyway?"

"Bottled up," said Chameleon, waving.
He stopped in front of the Pleasant Pickle Company.
Before he could knock, the door opened.

"THERE HE IS!" shouted the board members.
They carried Chameleon into the banquet room.

Balloons hung from the ceiling.

"Where is the formula?"
asked the Chairman of the Board.

Chameleon held up the wrinkled
paper. "Here it is!" he said proudly.

Everyone clapped.

"I'll copy it on the blackboard," said the
Chairman. "Let me have it." He read out loud:

"1 bushel cucumbers
(soaked in salty brine)
1 large horseradish
2 gallons vinegar
8 celery seeds
4 dill blossoms
and 1 cup mustard made with…
ah, with… ah…"

The Chairman paused. "GOOD HEAVENS!" he shouted.
"The writing at the bottom is blurred. The last
ingredient is missing!"

"MISSING?" cried everyone.

"Our secret formula is *worthless* without it!" groaned the Chairman. "What *shall* we do?"

"Ohhhhhhhhhhhhhhhhh!" sighed the board members.

A balloon popped.

"WAIT!" cried Chameleon.

He grabbed the secret formula, and lay across the bottom where the last line had been.

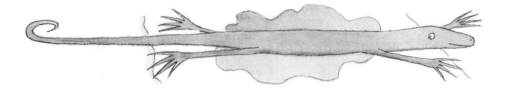

Spots and swirls flickered over his back.

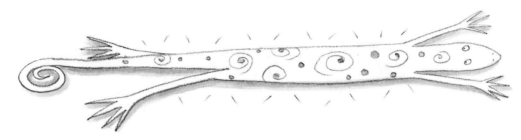

Dots and dashes flashed on and off, and then…

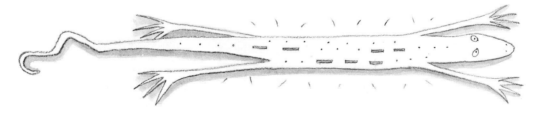

All at once…two words appeared, in large clear letters:

"Crinkleroot juice."

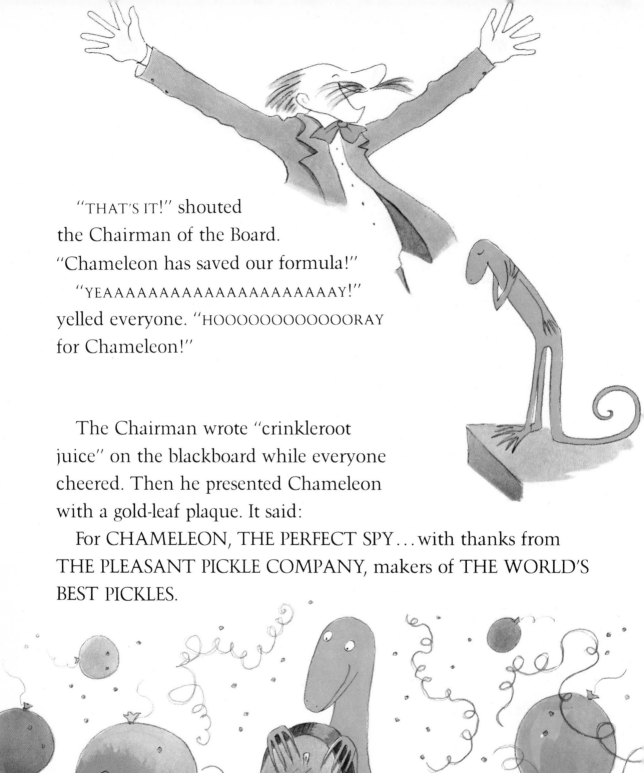

"THAT'S IT!" shouted
the Chairman of the Board.
"Chameleon has saved our formula!"

"YEAAAAAAAAAAAAAAAAAAAAY!"
yelled everyone. "HOOOOOOOOOOOORAY
for Chameleon!"

The Chairman wrote "crinkleroot
juice" on the blackboard while everyone
cheered. Then he presented Chameleon
with a gold-leaf plaque. It said:

For CHAMELEON, THE PERFECT SPY…with thanks from
THE PLEASANT PICKLE COMPANY, makers of THE WORLD'S
BEST PICKLES.